Inkbound

Jeff Coleman

Published internationally by Pallid Visions ®

PO box 5943

Buena Park, CA 90622, United States

Cover art and design ©2019 Vincent Chong (http://www.vincentchong-art.co.uk).

This book is a work of fiction. Any similarity between the characters and situations within its pages and places or persons, living or dead, is unintentional and coincidental.

For more information about the author, visit his homepage:
https://blog.jeffcolemanwrites.com/

ISBN 978-1-945997-14-3 (E-book)

ISBN 978-1-945997-15-0 (Hardcover)

ISBN 978-1-945997-16-7 (Paperback)

Library of Congress Control Number: 2019938906

First Edition.

Contents

Acknowledgments

This book is dedicated to my wife, my parents, and my patrons. You all have helped me out so much and in so many different ways. What else is there to say but "thank you!"

As is customary with all my books, I'd like to give a shout out to all of my patrons by name. If you became one after March 30, 2019, I'm sorry I wasn't able to list you here. But know that you, too, hold a special place in my heart, and that this book wouldn't have been possible without you.

Quiarrah

Jill Babbs

B.K.

Anthony Colannino

Voni Colannino

Jeannine Cook-Battles

Julia Davis

Christyne Demos

Alixevette Solstice

Angela Escarcega

Monica A. Franklin

Anna Garcia-Centner

Brandy Dalton

"JonBoy" Maddron

Susan Malloy

Pat Williamson

Allen Morris

Karen Palumar

Jessica Parkko

Janis Chandler

Melissa Iwata

Lisa Plante

Suzie Queen

Laura Anne StJohn

Karen Sutton

Rae Taylor

Chad Walker

Introduction

In 2015, my life changed forever. After packing a dark gray Samsonite suitcase with some of my more important belongings, I offered emotional farewells to my friends and family, gave up a stable nine-to-five job to become an independent contractor and, with passport in hand, boarded a one-way flight bound for the Philippines.

The reason for this crazy, foolhardy adventure? Love. Leaving everything behind for a chance at romance and your own personal happily-ever-after is, I think, one of the most cliché themes ever written. It's been the subject of far too many romance novels and films for me to count, and as such, I won't bore you with the details of that particular story. Suffice to say, with great risk comes great reward, and I'm happy to report that as of 2017, my life's journey has, through marriage, become beautifully and inextricably entangled with that of the most amazing person I've ever known.

But my happily-ever-after has not been without its challenges, and I've discovered that leaving everything behind to live as a guest in a foreign country isn't easy. Particularly challenging is the transition to the East from the West. Granted, the Philippines has been heavily influenced by Western culture, making that transition considerably easier for a spoiled American brat like myself. Still, there are cultural differences that, when combined with an acute case of homesickness, can make such an adjustment difficult.

Nevertheless, my time abroad has changed me for the better. I've witnessed some of the ways in which people are different— and much more importantly, I've witnessed many of the ways in which people are the same. I've been privileged to have the opportunity to live in the midst of a vibrant new culture, and through a process of osmosis, I've come to a fuller understanding and appreciation of the Filipino people.

I knew even before I arrived that I wanted to incorporate the Philippines into my writing. But I was afraid because I was a guest in a land I'd visited only twice prior to moving, and there was no way I could write with any confidence about a country I knew nothing about. So for a while, I resisted the urge to write and instead just *lived*, first in Manila, then in Bacolod. And by living, by processing my surroundings, I got to know the Philippines better. I made some friends. I learned how to hail a cab (a skill that's since been superseded by the introduction of the ride-hailing app, *Grab*). I even learned how to say a few things in Tagalog, as well as Ilonggo, my wife's native dialect.

Still, I wasn't confident in my ability to portray the Philippines accurately, and at first, I was only willing to dip my toes into the shallow end of the pool by writing a few short pieces of flash fiction. But eventually I realized that, while it would be impossible for me to get everything right (sometimes, I don't even think I get my own country right), I'd lived in the Philippines long enough that I could at least offer my readers a passingly authentic flavor, albeit from a foreigner's perspective.

Thus, *Inkbound* was born.

It is, with the utmost respect for the Filipino people, that I offer you this tale of Giles's journey, a story that, in some ways at least, mirrors my own. I've done my best to showcase the best of the Philippines, but neither have I shied away from difficult subjects, such as the ubiquitousness of poverty in that corner of the world. The character Norbing (who arguably steals the show, as you'll no doubt discover for yourself) is based on someone real, and while I never got to know him as well as I would have liked, I'd like to think that my highly romanticized and fanciful portrayal of who he might have been would make him smile. Like Norbing, he's an older gentleman who lacks the firm mastery of English that all younger Filipinos possess, which is why the dialogue is structured the way it is. You'll encounter a few Tagalog and Ilonggo words and phrases, most of which should be comprehensible to the English reader through context. But for those who prefer a more explicit translation, I've provided a glossary at the end of the book.

To my Filipino readers: Please forgive whatever mistakes I might have made. I've had my wife and some of her family read this story for accuracy, but as a foreigner, I'll never understand the Philippines as well as you.

To everyone else: I hope you enjoy the story :) *Inkbound* is the prequel to at least three planned novels, so if you find yourself falling in love with Giles's tale and are hoping for more, stay tuned!

Jeff
March 2019

1

The first thing Giles learned about the Philippines was that it was hot and humid.

He'd known it was a tropical country and had learned in elementary school that the closer one lived to the equator, the hotter and more humid it became. But he couldn't possibly have appreciated just how truly hot and truly humid it would be until he was deplaning at 10:37 p.m., feeling like he'd just entered a world-sized pressure cooker. Sweat popped out of his skin and his shirt stuck to his back.

It was Giles's first time outside the United States. In fact, it was his first time outside California. The knowledge that he now stood on the other side of the world, away from everyone and everything he'd ever known, terrified him in a way he couldn't have articulated back home. He found himself grabbing the sides of the rickety ladder for support as he climbed off the plane, the huge jet engines rumbling beside him, and he felt as if the oppressive tropical heat were trying to push him back. *You're not welcome*, the hostile weather seemed to say. *Go home.* And if he could have, he would have. But a few months ago Giles had made a mistake, and now he was here to fix it.

He waited in line to hand in his health declaration card. Then he waited in line again to get his passport stamped. He waited for his luggage to pass by on the conveyor. Finally, he waited in one more line to clear customs. A long hour and a half later, he was dragging his dark gray Samsonite suitcase on wheels through the double-doored exit.

Though Giles was sleep deprived, his eyes remained wide open, soaking in every detail of his surroundings. Anytime he saw something move out of the corner of his eye, he would whirl around for a better look and his hand would shoot toward the black leather notebook and pen in his right pants pocket, as if not doing so put them in danger of disappearing.

The sweltering air of Manila embraced him once more as he stepped outside and scanned the crowd for his contact. In the distance, white taxis pulled in to pick up and drop off passengers, horns blaring. A porter passed by and asked if he could carry his luggage toward the parking lot. Startled, Giles staggered back into the wall and had to tell the man no twice before he walked away to help someone else. Finally, Giles spotted his name on a sign to the left, held up by a gray-haired Filipino. The man introduced himself and shook his hand.

"Good evening, sir. I Norbing. How is flight?" Norbing spoke in a clipped accent and donned a warm smile that might have been infectious if Giles hadn't been awake for almost twenty hours.

"What?"

"I say 'How is flight?'"

"Oh. Tiring." Giles found the bustling parking lot disorienting, and it was hard to pay attention.

"Don't worry," said Norbing, "I take care of you. I get taxi over there," he said, pointing toward the loading and unloading area, "and then we stay in hotel for night. Tomorrow, we fly to Bacolod."

Giles's heart backflipped. After waiting for so many months, he would, at last, be able to set things right. That was if he didn't screw up again. The notebook in his pocket seemed to pulse in response, and Giles reached for it once more.

Norbing took his luggage, told him to hang back while he negotiated with a taxi driver, and after a few panicked minutes of standing alone again, led him into the back seat, where he was at last surrounded by air conditioning and relative quiet. The exhaustion that had been pounding against his battered body finally broke through his defenses, and he was asleep even before he reached his hotel.

2

Giles has the man right where he wants him. He's not a man, of course—at least on the inside—but something much worse, something dangerous. As more than a man himself, Giles easily recognizes the creature for what it is. Trailing twenty or thirty feet behind, Giles watches as the man sits down at a bus stop and pulls out the *L.A. Times*.

He angles around to get a better view, and once the man is clearly within Giles's sights, he pulls out the leather notebook and pen he always keeps in his right pants pocket, opens to the next blank page, and begins to write.

It's a binding, something he's practiced a dozen times before in his own private language. Of course, the language isn't important, only that the meaning of the words is clear and concise enough to capture the creature's essence, to draw it out from the fabric of reality and into the pages of his notebook.

He starts with the more superficial details and works his way in, capturing all the nuances of the man's behavior as he thumbs through the pages of his newspaper. If Giles does his job properly, the man won't realize what's happened until the binding is nearly complete, and by then it will be too late.

The man is already starting to fade like the end of a silent film when Giles hears a horn, followed by the sound of two cars colliding, and he turns to gawk at the accident. His concentration is only compromised for a moment, but a moment is all it takes. When he turns back toward the bench, the man is gone.

Giles's heart stops and his mouth runs dry. It takes him a few moments to process what's happened, to truly appreciate how badly he's fucked up.

The man is gone. The man. Gone.

Oh, fuck.

Giles starts riffling through the notebook, checks to see if perhaps he's written enough to complete the binding after all. But of course, he hasn't. He can feel the man, floating between two realities, angry and disoriented.

What have I done?

He turns, and now the sun has gone down as if hours have passed in a matter of seconds. Behind him, an unseen entity gives chase. It's the man, closing in, and when he speaks, he speaks inside Giles's head.

You fucked up, Giles. You fucked up good.

Giles runs and runs, but he can't get away, and soon partially substantial hands are closing around his neck—

Giles woke with a start. For a moment, the darkness confirmed that the dream was real, that he would soon find himself unable to breathe, that the man he'd tried to bind would be hovering overhead, grinning as he strangled the life out of him.

But no, that was impossible. Giles awoke fully and remembered he was in a hotel room near the airport. He flicked on the lamp beside the bed, blinking against the sudden flood of incandescent light.

His eyes drifted involuntarily toward the notebook on the nightstand. He could feel the partially bound creature, both inside and out, closer now than it had felt back in the States. It gave off a faint hum, a vibration in the air that lay just on the edge of his perceptual awareness. Giles took a deep breath.

In another room beside him, thought Giles, Norbing was most likely sleeping. It brought him some comfort, knowing that he wasn't alone. The man was like Giles, both human and Immortal—what their kind referred to as Earthbound—and that made them brothers. Their cultural backgrounds might have been wildly divergent, but in all the ways that mattered, they were the same.

Giles thought he wouldn't be able to fall asleep again, that he'd stay up the rest of the night haunted by the dream. But the weariness of a sleepless seventeen-hour flight had sunk in bone-deep, and it wasn't long before he was asleep once more.

3

One advantage of not sleeping on the airplane and arriving in the middle of the night was that Giles adjusted almost instantly to the new time zone. He yawned. Stretched. Turned over onto his side.

The dream from last night still tugged at him, tainting what would otherwise have been the start of a lovely day. He was troubled not just by the fear it had elicited but by the shame of the memory that had replayed before his sleeping eyes. He should have been more careful. He'd grown too comfortable, too confident to regard his job with the gravity it required. An Earthbound that was serious about his work would never have let the car accident distract him. But Giles knew he wasn't good enough for this job, just like he hadn't been good enough for Dad. Would he ever stop fucking up?

The creature he'd attempted to capture and later dreamed about, yanked from its bodily anchor but not having been bound entirely to the notebook, had fled through the layers of the world. Where a being in such a state ultimately ended up seemed randomly chosen, though none of the other Earthbound could say for sure. Partial bindings weren't something that happened often, and they had little knowledge of the phenomena.

What they did know was that the creature would have found another anchor, most likely a place, but possibly a person or an object, anything that could be inhabited and possessed. Quite often, believers in the supernatural would mistake such phenomena for the presence of a ghost, and in fact, this was how Giles had learned of the creature's location.

His brethren kept their ears to the ground, and when they heard credible rumors of possessions or hauntings, they investigated them.

If the rumor was real, if it turned out to be one of the creatures their race was sworn to bind, word would spread through a vast international network of Libraries—local repositories dedicated to keeping and guarding these imprisoned creatures—until the Earthbound who'd initiated the binding could be found and sent to complete it.

He glanced at his phone, which sat on the nightstand alongside his notebook and pen, and saw that it was already past ten. Fortunately, his connecting flight to Bacolod wasn't until three fifteen, and their hotel was only twenty minutes from the airport. He would still have time to shower and eat before moving on to his final destination.

"Good morning, sir," said Norbing when he arrived downstairs for breakfast.

"Morning."

"Sleep well?" Norbing's tone was bright and cheery. He piled a forkful of rice and some kind of sausage into his mouth.

"Yeah."

Norbing gestured toward the free buffet. "Get breakfast," he said, shoveling more meat and rice down his gullet. "Try longganisa."

Giles picked up a scoop of scrambled eggs, white rice, a couple of longganisa—they turned out to be the breakfast sausages Norbing was eating—and a cup of pineapple juice. There were other items as well: a red alien-looking fruit with thin green hairs called rambutan, sliced mangoes, and something called sisig. But he was too preoccupied with what he had to do to feel very hungry.

"Longganisa good," observed Norbing, pointing toward his plate. "Eat with rice."

He was right, Giles thought after trying some. It was just a little sweet and had a pleasant porky flavor. Maybe he was hungry after all.

"My favorite," said Norbing. "Parents make it every Sunday on farm." His eyes glazed over a little, assuming a faraway cast.

"What was it like," asked Giles, "growing up on a farm?"

"Busy," said Norbing, and his eyes seemed to withdraw even

further. "Always busy. Lot of chores. No school. Too much to do on farm.

"Was very hard. Youngest of seven children. We no get along. Liked to be alone and they tease me. They always say, *Gadinamgo nga bugtaw*, always make faces and hit me when parents not looking. We inherit farm when we older, but I no want to be farmer. All I want is draw."

"Is that your medium? Drawing?" Every one of the Earthbound worked through a particular medium, their own private means of binding the dangerous creatures that roamed the world in secret. There were writers, sculptors, painters, even musicians. The medium didn't matter, only that the work be expressive enough of the creature's nature to capture its essence.

"*Oo*," said Norbing, nodding in the affirmative. "I draw everything. Sky, bird, carabao, even family when they no looking. I try so hard, do best to learn, try to be better artist. I try—" Norbing paused, either attempting to find the words or struggling to translate them into English. "How do I say, want to make real…"

"You tried to capture their essence," said Giles, understanding perfectly. "You tried to reproduce every detail."

"*Oo*. Spend hours drawing, but parents get mad. Say I no good worker, say I no inherit farm with brothers if I no work hard."

Giles hadn't realized how difficult life could be for others of his kind. True, he'd been picked on in school for being different, and he'd had family problems of his own, given that Dad had run out on him and Mom when Giles was only seven. He'd felt responsible at the time, as if something he'd done as a child had disappointed and driven Dad away, and he'd spent hours locked in his room with the lights off, brooding in guilty silence as he pondered what he could have done differently to make him stay.

But Mom had accepted him for who he was—or, at least, for who she thought he was. He'd never told her about his true nature—that was something only the Earthbound themselves could comprehend—nor had she suspected that he was anything more than human. But she knew Giles wasn't like other children, that he had unusual interests, that he tended to be quiet, and that he preferred to keep to himself. Only instead of assuming there was something wrong with him and trying to fix it, she'd taken the time to get to know him better and provided the freedom he needed to become more fully himself. It was a tragedy Norbing hadn't experienced that same kind of acceptance.

"When older, I feel different. Not like others. I—" He paused again. "My English no good."

"It's okay," said Giles, "I know what you're trying to say."

Giles knew because he'd been through it himself. The feeling that you weren't yourself, that your humanity was only a part of what you were, that just beneath the flesh and blood exterior there was something foreign, something the human part of yourself couldn't understand but was forced to accept. Giles had experienced hints of his dual nature since childhood, like the partial abstract memories of a time before Earth existed that would sometimes flash through his head unbidden, too strange and insistent to be just an ordinary daydream; or the shadow of a vast and ancient knowledge that always hovered over the periphery of his perception, yet remained forever out of reach; or the stubborn, absolute certainty that there was more to the world than what he could perceive through the five human senses alone. But it wasn't until he was an adolescent that the Immortal half of his nature really started to haunt him, and by then it had almost torn him apart.

Norbing nodded, staring down for a moment at the wood-grain surface of the table. "Was hard," he said more softly. "Getting angrier, more confused, more frustrated. Had to go into world, discover who I am. Have big fight with father. He disown me. Throw me out. Tell me never come back.

"I live on street with squatters. Was robbed. Have no money, no food, but I still try to draw, try to find simple jobs so I have money for paper and pencil. All I want is draw, even if I hungry, if I only eat few times a week.

"Then a woman, Ms. Mylene, she find me on street. She know what I am, take me in, clean me, feed me, teach me what I am. She like mother. Very hard when she die."

Giles wondered how many others were out there in the world like Norbing had been, homeless, perhaps never discovering what they were. Maybe, without help, their dual nature had driven them mad. Giles felt truly blessed for the support his mom had given him growing up, and he decided that when he returned home he would tell her how much he loved her.

"I try contact family. No phone on farm, but write letters. They never answer. Still don't know what happen to them, don't know if brothers still alive."

"That's terrible," said Giles, and he began to fidget, suddenly uncertain and self-conscious because he wasn't sure what he could say to empathize with the man's struggles.

But then, just as Giles thought Norbing would cry, the man broke into an incandescent smile. "I happy now. I know who I am, know what my life for."

And then Giles could relate once more. That was how he'd felt when he finally learned the truth, when he was introduced to the Libraries and his purpose had finally unfurled before him like a late-blooming flower.

Of course, that was before the accident. Now, self-doubt gnawed at his insides, and he wondered if he would ever feel secure again.

"Norbing, did you ever make mistakes, ever do things you regretted?"

"*Oo.* I human, too."

"But did you ever do something *really* bad?" pressed Giles. "Something awful? Something that made you doubt you could ever do your job again?"

Norbing leaned back into his chair and looked up for a moment. Then he peered down at Giles as if gazing through him. "We all do bad things," said Norbing. "We Immortals, but we also human, and humans make mistakes. You young, you maybe too confident. So you make mistake. Now you own mistake, and you fix mistake, and next time you be careful because you remember mistake."

"I hope so."

"You will," said Norbing. "You Immortal, too." The man looked down at Giles's plate and *tsked*. "You eat now. I get you more longganisa," and before Giles could protest, Norbing was already at the buffet counter, picking up more rice and sausage.

4

After breakfast, Giles and Norbing returned to their rooms to pack. Giles showered and changed. He glanced at the notebook once more, feeling the creature's half-presence just beyond its surface, then placed it firmly in his pants pocket.

They met downstairs at almost a quarter past twelve. Norbing hailed a taxi and, before long, they were heading for the airport. Giles watched buildings streak past the windows, one after the other. He was surprised by how many American companies there were. Burger King, McDonalds, Pizza Hut, Starbucks, even 7-Eleven.

Norbing turned his signature smile on Giles, and this time Giles tried his best to return the gesture.

"How you like Manila?"

"It's interesting."

"You like Bacolod," said Norbing, clasping his hands together. "Not as big as Manila, but good food. You try chicken inasal!"

"I will." But Giles found it difficult to think about food.

"You be fine," said Norbing, reading him like a book. "You care about job. You want to do well, so you will."

Giles didn't reply. His Library had said much the same: that he was young, that he meant well, that he would learn from his mistakes and shouldn't be too hard on himself. But Giles couldn't shake the feeling that he was about to screw up again, that the rest of his career would be one long and unending parade of fuck-ups.

You fucked up, Giles, he heard the voice from his dream say. *You fucked up good.*

"Be confident," Norbing warned. "It sense you. It know when you afraid and make you more afraid. Need to believe you can win. Need to fight fear."

Giles thought of his dream once more and wondered if the creature in the notebook had been responsible for it. "I'll try."

"You no try," said Norbing. "You do."

Giles settled into the backseat, trying not to let the heat get the best of him. The word *aircon* had been painted on the outside of the car, but when they'd gotten in, the driver had told them the A/C was broken.

Even with so many American companies around him, Giles keenly felt the distance between the Philippines and California. Manila was different enough to unsettle him and similar enough to make him homesick.

One difference Giles found particularly jarring was the ubiquity of poverty on this side of the world. He'd seen plenty of homeless people back in California, especially in Los Angeles, sprawled out on park benches or standing on street corners with signs promising work in exchange for food. But here it was so much worse. There were families living beneath bridges and huddled against buildings, entire streets lined with squatters, all living in flimsy, dilapidated shanty houses that seemed like they might collapse at any moment. Many of these squatter homes had been raised right beside expensive condos and restaurants. Most heartbreaking of all were the children, who approached stationary cars at every red light in soiled rags, begging for coins. Giles couldn't imagine growing up under such squalid conditions.

On the road, cars and motorcycles wove in and out of lanes in time to the irregular staccato beat of honking horns, while pedestrians thought nothing of crossing the street in the middle of heavy traffic as if the road were just a busy sidewalk. Giles had thought Los Angeles traffic was bad, but Manila was in a class all its own.

A strange gaudily ornamented vehicle that looked like the lovechild of a bus and a jeep swerved in front of them, belching out a plume of acrid black smoke. The taxi driver slammed on his brakes, muttering something that sounded to Giles like *"Hi nakoo,"* and exchanged frustrated words with Norbing in

Tagalog.

"What's that?" asked Giles.

"Jeepney," said Norbing.

Then, with a hand pressed to the notebook in his pocket, Giles experienced a sudden, unexpected surge of anxiety—*What if I can't do this?*—and had to take a deep, calming breath.

He could feel the partially bound creature inside and, for the first time he wondered if that awareness flowed both ways. Could it read him? Was it trying to make him more unsure, trying to make him fail?

These creatures could reach into people's minds to discover their darkest secrets, their most private internal struggles, then drag them out into the light of the conscious mind, amplifying people's pain and suffering until there was no room left for anything else. They fed on negative emotions—like empathic vampires, feasting on humanity's anguish and distress, and people often died by their hand. Once, long ago, in a universe much like Earth's, they'd consumed almost everything, and had nearly brought the fabric of existence to its knees. The Immortals (not Earthbound, not yet) had thwarted them, imprisoned them someplace where they hoped they would never bother anyone again. But a number of them had escaped and fled, taking on physical form in order to evade detection.

That was the reason people like Giles existed, to hunt them down, to imprison them so they could never again wreak the kind of havoc that had once destroyed almost everything. Giles supposed there must also be Immortals bound to non-human forms on other worlds and in other universes, but he knew nothing about that, not in his current incarnation.

"We here," said Norbing as the car pulled up to the curb.

Giles started, surprised. At some point he'd zoned out and hadn't realized where he was.

Norbing handed the taxi driver 250 pesos, grumbling that the fare shouldn't have been more than 125, then wound around to the trunk and grabbed Giles's luggage.

"It's okay," said Giles, climbing out of the car, "I can get that."

But Norbing only smiled. "I get it. I not that old yet."

NAIA 3 was much smaller than the international terminal where he'd deplaned after arriving from the States, and all of its gates fit into a room about half the size of a football field. They checked in at the Cebu Pacific counter, passed through security, and sat beside their gate. Twenty minutes later, a voice blared from the overhead speaker in both English and Tagalog, alerting waiting passengers that Cebu Pacific flight 5J 481 bound for Bacolod was now boarding.

"You like Bacolod," said Norbing again as they handed their boarding passes to a woman in a bright yellow uniform.

Giles patted the notebook in his pocket for comfort, then followed Norbing up the ramp.

5

Giles leaned back in his seat and allowed himself to be consumed by the heavy thrum of the jet engine. Once, about fifteen minutes into the flight, a stewardess passed by with a cart offering drinks and snacks. When she came to his row, he politely declined, then settled back and closed his eyes.

He began to doze, and the airplane seat beneath him transformed into the easy chair he'd been sitting on when Dad had hugged him for the last time. He'd said in his British accent that he was going on a trip, but promised to be back soon. Seven-year-old Giles waited nine months before giving up on his return. *What did I do wrong?* It was a question that would occur to him many times. By then, he'd withdrawn into himself completely and, having been a loner for most of his short life, the teasing at school intensified, so that all he wanted to do was stay in bed and let the day pass over him like a drifting cloud.

Then Giles was back up in the air once more, not in an airplane but flying, soaring through the sky, where he at last felt free. There was another world out there, his true home. He only had to reach out and seize it.

Then he was accepting a leather notebook from one of his colleagues at the Library. They'd taken him under their wing. They'd explained who and what he was and had finally given him purpose at a time in his life when he had very nearly driven himself mad. The notebook was as much a savior as it was a gift, and that night he held it close to his breast like a lover, not knowing the weight, the burden it would represent when he finally began to use it.

Then Giles was watching the man, sitting at the bus stop, and again Giles watched himself fail, watched the man flee. A voice drifted up to him through the layers of his mind, a sneering, contemptuous sound.

You fucked up, Giles. You fucked up good.

Then there was a crash and a sudden shuddering clatter, and Giles snapped awake.

Inside his pocket, the notebook had grown warm. A panicked thought occurred to him.

I can't do this.

"Ladies and gentlemen," said a woman over the intercom, "we're experiencing turbulence and ask that you please remain seated with your seat belts fastened. Thank you."

Giles looked around. Norbing was next to him, still fast asleep. He gazed out the window, occasionally placing his hand in his pocket to check on the notebook. Would he fuck up again? Giles knew how to complete the binding, but he was still afraid. He should have gotten it right the first time. The fact that he was in this position at all made him question whether he would be able to fix it when the time came.

When they finally landed, he sighed and tapped Norbing on the shoulder.

"We're here."

They waited for the door to open, then headed out into the late-afternoon heat.

6

They arrived in Bacolod a little past four p.m., and by 4:45 they were pulling up in a white taxi to a small house in a barangay on Burgos Ave. Norbing paid the driver, grabbed Giles's bag, and got out to open a large wrought-iron gate.

"This my home," said Norbing. "You stay and rest. Then tomorrow you fix mistake."

Giles wasn't sure if it was better to wait or get it over with now, so he deferred to the wisdom of his host.

Giles thought he'd gotten a good taste of the Philippines in Manila, but Bacolod turned out to be very different. On the way to Norbing's house from Silay Airport, they'd passed mile after mile of sugarcane fields, a few of them on fire. The bright orange flames and thick gray smoke had frightened him until Norbing explained that they were controlled fires and that it was the way the farmers cleared their fields for the next crop. Where downtown Manila was crammed to capacity with high-rise towers, Bacolod was smaller and dominated primarily by strip malls and single-story buildings. If Manila had felt like another country, Bacolod felt, in some ways at least, like another world.

"We have lunch now," said Norbing. "There lechon in fridge."

There were three rooms inside the house, a combined living room and kitchen, a bathroom, and a bedroom, and there was no central air conditioning, something Giles would have considered a necessity back in the States. Outside, the house was surrounded by a tall hollow concrete block fence with shards of broken glass stuck into the top to dissuade intruders.

"Sorry," said Norbing. "Lechon from yesterday morning. Not so good."

"It's okay."

"Tomorrow, we have breakfast at good resto. I treat you."

Giles was touched by the man's generosity. They hadn't known each other until last night, yet Norbing had opened his home to him without a second thought. Giles had once heard that Filipinos were known for their hospitality. Norbing was proof that it was true.

"Thank you," said Giles.

"For what?"

"Everything. For picking me up, for booking my hotel, for taking me into your home."

Norbing gave him an easygoing smile. "It nothing," he said.

"My Library in Bacolod, they pay for everything." He winked, and Giles grinned.

"Then please, also tell them I said thank you."

They sat at a small table with two glasses of cold water, a half cup of rice each, and day-old lechon wrapped in tin foil. Norbing said that when it was fresh, the pig's skin was crunchy, and that the meat was juicier and more tender. But Giles proved to be easy to please. He'd never had pork like this back in the States.

"It's really good," said Giles.

"Cebu have best lechon. You come back sometime and try."

When they were finished eating, they sat in companionable silence, while outside jeepneys and tricycles honked and sputtered along the road.

"Do you still work?" asked Giles after a while, breaking the silence.

"*Oo*, but I retire soon. I work long time. Want rest."

"What will you do then?"

"I draw," said Norbing, smiling. "No binding, just drawing. Want to make art, like my father no let me do."

Giles thought it was interesting that both he and Norbing had been forced to deal with less-than-stellar fathers. Both men, for one reason or another, had been unable or unwilling to support their children. *Dad,* he thought, feeling an all-too-familiar ache in his chest, *why wasn't I good enough for you?*

"I glad I leave," Norbing continued. "My father no good for me. If I stay, he make me farmer. But I no want to be farmer, I Earthbound."

For a moment, Giles wondered: *Am I better off without Dad?*

But all this talk about bad fathers was making Giles depressed, and he shuttered that part of his mind and glanced around the room, hoping to change the subject. It was a simple, homey space, and he imagined Norbing must have all he needed right here. He noticed a series of photos on the wall, many with what looked like a younger version of Norbing standing or sitting beside a woman.

"Did you marry?" It wasn't common, not for the Earthbound, but occasionally it happened.

"*Oo*," said Norbing. "But she die nine years ago. Now I live alone."

"I'm sorry."

"It okay," said Norbing. "She at peace now. We in love, but we also fight. She no understand me, and I keep many secret."

Giles could see how having to hide a fundamental aspect of your nature would put a strain on a marriage. It wasn't just the fact that they had to go out into the world and capture dangerous supernatural beings that other humans didn't know existed. It was that their humanity was only a part of what they were.

It was as if the human world existed in two dimensions, and

while most were unaware of a third dimension, the Earthbound understood that it existed and that a whole other universe spun along its axis. Yet they were bound to the same two-dimensional space as everyone else. That hidden third dimension cast a dark shadow over their lives, a haunting reminder of all they'd given up to keep the cosmos safe. Because of this, the Earthbound were possessed by the perennial need for solitude and silent reflection, desperate for time to contemplate a world that would be out of reach for the entirety of their Earthly lives. It was the reason why Giles couldn't see himself ever finding a partner.

"It's hard relating to people," said Giles. "I've never been in a relationship myself. I've always had trouble just making friends." He recalled the inner turmoil that reached its peak by high school: the human half of his nature expressing its biological desire for companionship while the Immortal half of his nature pushed it away.

"It hard," said Norbing. "You want love, but you also want to be alone. I spend many hours alone, and wife always complain. Say I no love her, say I selfish, that all I want is draw. I try so hard to show her I love her, but it never enough. But we happy, too." Norbing smiled, and once more his eyes took on a faraway look.

"She take care of Ms. Mylene before she die. Her name Anna. She nurse. She so nice. She care for Ms. Mylene. I fall in love with her and ask her marry." Norbing smiled and focused back on Giles. "Maybe someday you too find love."

"Maybe," but Giles doubted it very much.

"Did you have any children?" Among the pictures, Giles had spotted an infant.

Norbing hung his head slightly, and his smile faded. "*Oo*, one. But she sick and die when only baby. Wife no want more."

The sadness behind the man's eyes tugged at Giles's heart-strings. "I'm sorry."

"It long time ago. Sometimes I wonder what she like if older, what life be like if she alive. But maybe she no like me, maybe sometimes she feel I no love her like mother. I don't know."

"I'm sure she would've loved you very much," said Giles. "You're kind and generous. Any child would be lucky to have you for a father."

"Thank you," said Norbing, and the smile rebounded.

After a while, Norbing rose from the table. "I take nap. You rest, too. Need strength. You take bedroom."

Norbing headed for the couch but Giles tried to stop him.

"I can take the couch," said Giles. "It's your house."

"And you guest," said Norbing. "You take bed. Couch is fine. Very comfortable." He pushed down on the cushion with his right hand as if to demonstrate.

Giles protested further, but Norbing wasn't having any of it, and finally Giles conceded, thanked him, and headed for the bedroom.

"Air conditioner in window," called Norbing over Giles's shoulder. "Make sure to close door."

So, there was an air conditioner after all. He cranked the dial to seven and sighed contentedly as a gust of cold air whooshed around his head and shoulders. He located the bed, a small single mattress with dark brown sheets and a single pillow, and plopped down on top of it.

As he lay on his back, he began to think. He reflected on the job he would have to do tomorrow, on whether he was up for the task or not, on his life back home, on how much he missed Mom. His heart ached for Norbing, whose life was mired in so much anguish. Giles was glad the man had found happiness in spite of it.

He reached into his pocket, pulled out the notebook—the creature partially contained within was almost quivering now—and held it before the dim light of the curtained window.

Giles wondered if he'd volunteered for this in a prior existence, or if his fate had been chosen for him. He certainly couldn't remember asking for it. His job came with so much responsibility, sacrifice, and pain. Though their work remained unrecognized, the Earth's continued existence hinged on their efforts to bind the preternatural terrors that, if left to their own devices, would consume everything. In a very real way, Giles and his kind carried the weight of the world on their shoulders. But he couldn't say it was a bad life, because what Norbing had said was true: he'd discovered his reason for being and was living it. Things might be hard, but he led a purpose-driven life and was working toward the common good of all, something that fulfilled him in a way nothing else could have.

Life was bizarre, he thought. Many believed that if they could know the mind of God, they would finally be able to make sense of everything. But Giles, by virtue of his dual nature, possessed at least a small understanding of life's mysteries, and he found his knowledge only served to confuse matters further.

He lay like that for an hour, perhaps two, watching as the sunlight filtering through the curtain transformed first from white to gold, then to orange and red. Eventually, his eyelids drooped and awareness faded, sputtered, expired.

Beside him on the mattress, the notebook waited.

7

Once more, Giles has the creature right where he wants him, and once more, just before he can commit its essence to the pages of his notebook, he's distracted by the accident. When he looks up, the creature is gone.

Giles riffles through the pages, as if he can somehow go back in time to finish the job through sheer willpower alone. But no matter how many times he checks, it's not there, not entirely, and he knows he's fucked up good.

A starless night descends over the world like a burial cloth, and Giles again senses the creature behind him, pursuing. Giles runs, tries to get away, because if he isn't fast enough, the creature will catch up to him and kill him, only—

Why should I bother? The creature asks in a soundless voice that echoes inside Giles's head. *You're no threat. You're too weak. If you try, you'll only fail as you did before.*

"No!" shouts Giles. His voice tapers, damped by the darkness around him. "I'll get you." But deep down, Giles doubts it. He wonders if the creature is right, if he'll just fail again.

I'm a fuckup, he thinks to himself. *Why do I bother trying?*

Inaudible laughter reverberates inside his head. *You fucked up, Giles. You fucked up good.* And just like that, the presence that was pursuing him disappears.

Giles feels oddly abandoned. "Come back," he shouts, turning backward, his face tilted up toward endless black. "Come back, you coward!"

"I'm so disappointed in you."

Giles whirls around as another man emerges, walking toward him from across the street. He stares at Giles with cold, disgusted eyes, and it takes Giles a moment to realize who this other man is.

"I always knew you'd be a fuckup," says Dad, stopping a dozen paces away, as if he can't bear to come any closer.

Giles tries to speak, but his throat has closed tight like a rusty hatch, and all he can manage is a low keening moan.

"Don't look at me like that," says Dad before turning away so that Giles can only see the back of his head. "It's pathetic. Why do you think I left you and your mother in the first place?"

All the insecurities Giles experienced as a child and never quite got over as an adult wash over him at once, an agonizing flash flood of emotion.

"Mom said you couldn't handle being a father, that it wasn't my fault. She said I shouldn't blame myself—"

"Bullshit." Dad spits the word with such contempt that Giles takes an involuntary step back. "You were such a whiny little brat, always moping around the house. You could never do anything right. You were a failure as a child, and now, you're a failure as an adult."

Deep down, Giles always believed Dad's decision to abandon them had been his fault, that somehow he must have done something so terrible that Dad couldn't bring himself to stay. But Giles never expected to confront him like this, never expected to hear confirmation of the truth from the man's own lips.

Dad turns to face him once more, his face a mask of frosty indifference, and proclaims, "You fucked up, Giles. You fucked up good."

It's the last thing Dad says before he disappears.

Alone in the dark, Giles sinks to his knees, crying, head hidden between his legs just like the seven-year-old child who lost his father so many years ago.

"Dad, come back," he cries between sobs. "I promise, I'll do better." But his plea disappears into the dark. "I can do it! I'll bind it this time, I swear." Giles, however, hears the weakness in his voice and realizes he doesn't really believe it.

Once more, Giles woke with a start. In the distance, a

rooster crowed. He reached for his phone and glanced down at the display. Three seventeen a.m. He sighed, wiping sweat from his brow, and pulled himself up into a sitting position. He could feel the notebook pulsing on the mattress beside him as if it were alive, and he supposed that in a sense it was.

Dad. Giles felt something in the pit of his stomach, a wrenching, gut-twisting pull he hadn't felt in years. He'd tried so hard growing up to be good, to be worthy of Dad's love. Secretly, he used to wish that Dad would return one day, discover he'd grown up to be a successful adult, and decide to stick around after all. A fool's hope, but Giles had centered his entire adolescent life around it just the same. Only he'd screwed everything up, and he was sure that if Dad knew anything of him now, he'd only hang his head and say he'd always known Giles would turn out to be a fuckup.

Giles took a deep, shuddering breath. The notebook beside him was writhing now, uncoiling from its binding like a compressed spring, and Giles had to get himself under control. He couldn't remember every detail of the dream, only bits and pieces, but somehow he knew his mind had been replaying that ill-fated memory, that the creature must have been inside his head as well, playing off his insecurities, trying to break his resolve.

Norbing's voice floated up from the ether of his bleary, semiconscious memory. *It sense you. It know when you afraid, make you more afraid.*

Though a rational part of Giles did its best to assert control over the sudden rush of negative emotions, he found himself seized by a panic that bordered on hysteria. He couldn't do this. The creature and his father were right: he was a failure. People would get hurt, maybe die, and it would be all his fault.

He grabbed the notebook, opened it, and poured over the pages. He'd been so damn close! He'd nearly captured it. Why had he been so fucking stupid? He couldn't even complete a simple binding. He was worthless.

When Norbing knocked on the door at seven thirty to tell him it was time for breakfast, Giles was still frantically flipping through the pages.

8

"Eat," said Norbing between mouthfuls of sisig. "Need strength."

They'd walked across the street to a small, partially enclosed roadside stand called Norma's Eatery, where jeepney and taxi drivers stopped for meals.

Giles stared down at the tapsilog in front of him—beef, garlic rice, and a fried sunny-side-up egg—pushing grains of rice around the plate with his fork while a queasy, anxious feeling wormed around inside his stomach.

I can't do this. Fuck, I can't do this.

He could feel the tremor of the creature in the notebook, resonating with his own insecurities and magnifying them.

"I can't do this," said Giles out loud. "Norbing, I can't do this."

"Stop," said Norbing, his voice hard as steel. It hit Giles like a slap. "You no doubt, you *can* do it, you *will* do it. Say it."

"Say what?"

"Say I *will* do it. Say now."

"I will do it," said Giles in a hollowed-out voice. "I'll catch it."

"Yes," said Norbing, "You will."

And after a moment his panic began to subside. It didn't go away, not completely, but the emotion dwindled to more tolerable levels. Beneath all his fear and uncertainty, Giles once more felt the creature's own fear, radiating off the notebook in thick, undulating waves. Yes, Giles realized, it was desperate. There was nothing it could do, nowhere it could run, and it was doing whatever it could to prevent Giles from completing his assignment. Giles took a deep breath.

"You were right. I can feel it inside my head, chiseling away at me, trying to take advantage of my weaknesses. I'm scared, Norbing."

"It okay to be scared," said Norbing, "As long as you do job anyway."

Giles finally took a bite of his breakfast. "This is good," he said. Norbing had taught him the Filipino way to eat just about any dish, a bit of the main course paired with a forkful of rice.

"My favorite resto," said Norbing, smiling. "Good food."

Giles hadn't been sure what to think until he'd tried it. Now he was a believer. Gems, he thought, often hid in the most unexpected places.

He fanned himself with his free hand. It was only 8:22 in

the morning, and already the temperature was climbing into the eighties. And it was so damn humid. Norbing had told him the weather was coolest November through February, only about twenty-one to twenty-three degrees Celsius (or seventy to seventy-three degrees Fahrenheit, he'd determined after some quick Googling.) But it was only mid-October and still uncomfortably hot, and he lamented the fact that he would be going home before he could experience much of the better weather. At least they hadn't been hit by a typhoon.

After a few moments of silence, Norbing called out to the woman running the stand—"*Dai*"—and when she looked up, he drew a rectangle in the air with his fingers.

"What does that mean?"

"Bill out."

Sure enough, the woman came with a tiny slip of paper in a bamboo basket. She said something to him in Ilonggo. He laughed, said something in response with a wink and a nod, then reached into his pocket and produced 150 pesos.

"*Salamat*," said Norbing when the woman came back with change. Then to Giles: "We go now. We have thing to catch. Remember, you can do it, you *will* do it. Say again."

"I will catch it," said Giles, this time with a little more confidence. But then he fingered the notebook in his pocket, and he felt his doubt creep back once more.

9

Norbing gave Giles a ride in his tricycle, wending through a series of small narrow side streets. It was little more than a rickety steel sidecar welded to a low-cost motorcycle, and it clanged, jittered, and sputtered as Norbing snaked and swerved around the cars in front of him. It was Giles's first time in such a vehicle, and for a moment he forgot about the creature partially bound inside his pocket.

It's a death trap.

"Is this safe?" asked Giles, raising his voice above the noise of the lawn-mower-like engine.

Norbing laughed. "*Oo.*"

Finally, they pulled up to the curb outside a rundown three-story apartment building, flanked on both sides by flimsy squatter constructions. Outside the front entrance, coarse brown rope blocked the entryway, along with a wooden sign with the words, "Danger. Keep Out." printed in red paint.

Giles could feel an invisible darkness cloying to the building, pulsing to the same frequency as the notebook.

I can't do this, thought Giles, while inside his pocket he could feel the creature beating like a perpetually startled heart. It was champing at the bit to get away but didn't have the strength to flee in its diminished form.

"This is it, isn't it?"

"*Oo*," said Norbing, looking up into the windows on the upper floors. "It abandoned now. After creature attach to building, woman kill herself, jump out three-story window. Library know local government, get building closed down. Residents told gas leak."

"Someone already *died*?" Guilt began to circulate through his system like blood poisoning.

It's my fault. I lost focus, the creature escaped, and it killed *someone.*

Of course, the woman had killed herself, but there was no doubt as to who was the truly responsible party. The creature had fed off her negative emotions, enlarging them, until all that was left of her mind was a rotting, aching despair that longed for the peace of death. She'd been as good as pushed, and it was because of Giles's failure that the creature had gotten to her.

Norbing must have noticed a change in his features because the man grabbed his shoulders and shook him hard until he turned and they were face to face.

"Not your fault," said Norbing firmly. "Say it. *Not my*

fault."

"It's not my fault," but Giles didn't really believe it.

"*Sige*. Say again. *Not my fault.*"

"It's not my fault."

"*Sige*. Good. You go in there and you bind it. You no let it get to you, you no let it take control."

"Okay," said Giles, letting himself off the tricycle.

"You can do it," said Norbing. "You *will* do it. Say it."

"I will do it."

"Good," said Norbing. "Good luck."

"Thanks."

Giles pushed aside the rope and walked inside.

10

Giles ascended a staircase in the dark. There were two layers of dark, the first an absence of light—the windows had all been shuttered—and the second an absence of substance as if all the colors of the world had faded to a dull black-and-white shadow. That second darkness swelled as Giles made his way upstairs.

The notebook in his pocket was vibrating now, humming like a high-voltage wire. Without thinking, he reached into his pocket and rested his fingers on the electrically charged surface.

I killed someone. The thought rang through his head, drowning out everything else. *I killed someone, and it's my fault.*

Then came Dad's voice, echoing from the ashes of a partially remembered dream: *You fucked up, Giles. You fucked up good.*

Guilt pressed him, wrung him repeatedly like a worn-out rag.

I want to die.

He deserved it, he thought. In fact, just then, he believed

death was too good for him, that perhaps damnation was better.

A sign on the wall revealed that he had reached the second floor. Giles pressed on.

"What's the point?" Dad's accusing voice continued inside his head. "You couldn't complete a simple binding the first time. What makes you think you can pull this off now? You might as well pack up your things and go home."

"No," whispered Giles. "I can't." He couldn't back out now. A woman had died because of his mistake, and he couldn't face the very real possibility that if he didn't try, more could die.

Besides, behind the guilt, behind the extreme fear of failure, behind even his father's disapproving voice, there was a part of his mind that remained clear, a place where he could recognize what the creature was doing to him. It was trying to overwhelm him, trying to push him over the edge so that he would feel he had no choice but to give up. In this corner of his mind, he sensed how terrified and desperate the creature was and how hard it was pushing back against him. Even in its purgatorial half state, it didn't want him to complete the binding and remove it from the world.

Norbing had been right: he needed to be strong. He couldn't let the creature get to him, couldn't let it break him down. If he let his guard down, even for a moment, it would squeeze the life out of him, and then he would fail for sure.

Giles was finally approaching the third floor. By now, the

world felt so hollow and thin that he was reminded of when Dad had taken him and Mom up to Holcomb Valley in the San Bernardino Mountains. At an altitude of 7,500 feet, the air was thin and insubstantial, and Giles had felt like throwing up.

"You always were a baby," mocked Dad.

Giles closed his eyes and bit back tears. He knew the voice wasn't real, but it was so goddamn painful to hear all the flaws he'd always believed about himself, to hear all the reasons he'd imagined Dad had walked out on them. A wave of anguish ripped through him, but he did his best to shove it aside and continued walking.

After climbing stairs that seemed never-ending, he approached the landing on the third floor.

"You can't do this," said Dad. "You're a failure. You're just going to fuck up again."

"Quiet," whispered Giles, passing through the hall and scanning the various doors. He didn't know in which room the creature had taken up residence, but he was able to home in on it based on what he could feel coming from the notebook. So close to the creature's essence, it responded to the smallest changes in distance, pulsing hard when he came closer and trailing off when he grew more distant. He gradually narrowed it down, until at last he was standing before room 307, certain he'd found what he was looking for.

There, on the other side of that door, was the hiding place

the creature had fled to after Giles made his mistake, where it had driven a poor woman to commit suicide, where it would likely drive more toward a similar fate if he didn't nip this in the bud now. Would he have the strength to slog through the painful emotions the creature was trying to drown him with? Would he find the focus necessary to complete the binding? He didn't know, but he knew he had to try.

"Don't go in there," Dad warned.

Taking a deep breath, Giles grabbed the knob and threw open the door.

11

The room was dark and dingy, with old torn furniture pushed against the walls. Swirling motes of dust funneled downward in narrow shafts of light beneath the cracks in the drawn window shades. Without needing to be told, Giles knew this was the window where the woman had jumped to her death. He could feel her despair, long after her death, swirling around the room alongside the dust. The darkness of it, a cold and empty void, suffocating, trying to push back the tiny bars of light that crept into the room through the bottom of the window.

That same void was now pushing against him, too, swelling, trying to bust through the protective walls he'd constructed inside his mind. He could feel the weakness in those walls; they were in danger of collapse. Dark, poisonous emotions surged through him, battering his defenses, but for now, at least, the walls held, and Giles focused on the job he had to do.

He reached into his pocket and pulled out the notebook, which by now was vibrating so forcefully he could feel it in his jaw. He pried it open, pausing on the page where he'd stopped mid-sentence all those months ago. He could no longer get a physical read on the creature, but he didn't need to now. He'd already gotten those superficial details. They'd been the first to be committed to paper, the smallest aspect of the creature's essence. What he needed was its soul, its corruption, its dark intentions, and he could feel those things so strongly now. He reached into his pocket again and produced a black pen.

What if I fail?

Another wave of dark emotions smashed into the mental wall, and he could feel it begin to give around the edges. The things he sensed, how could he hope to articulate such depth, a depth so complex that no words, human or divine, could hope to capture them? Another wave. Another crash. The mental partition creaked and groaned under the weight of the creature's attacks.

Never mind. He didn't have to get the description just right. It was a foolish fear, another of the creature's efforts to distract him. His job was not to express every detail, only to draw a crude approximation, something close enough to identify it, to call it by its true name, to draw it out of the world and into the pages of his notebook.

He lifted his pen and began to write.

Giles soon fell into a rhythm. He felt the creature being pulled out of the space, felt the room lighten, the darkness injecting into the pages of his notebook like swamp-black ink. Then there came a soundless shriek that rebounded inside his head.

I KNOW WHAT YOU ARE.

He ignored it, continued writing, and the darkness diminished. His progress encouraged him, helped him slip more confidently into his work.

YOU CAN'T DO THIS. YOU'LL FAIL JUST AS YOU DID BEFORE.

"I already am," whispered Giles. "Your time is up."

NOOOOOO!

The word transformed into a hurricane, swirling through his head, knocking him off balance. The darkness in the room swelled again until it was completely black, and when his eyesight returned a moment later, he saw the woman who'd died, lying facedown on the rotting couch. After a long breathless moment, the woman stirred. She turned her head toward Giles, and what he saw in her hideous features shocked him so much that he staggered back, the pen and notebook dropping to the floor beside him.

Her jaw had come unhinged and now hung slack from thick cords of moldering flesh that looked as if they'd soured beneath the hot Philippines sun. She stared at him with empty eye sockets, face twisted into a grotesque glower. *You did this to me,* her expression seemed to say, and Giles's stomach dropped out from under him.

"You did this," said Dad, who now stood beside the woman, turning his gaze back and forth between her and his failure of a son.

"You did this," Dad repeated, and this time his words were reinforced by a second soundless echo from the creature he was trying to bind. "This woman died because you failed."

Giles watched her fetid corpse rise from the couch.

"Your fault," said Dad.

Watched as she inched toward the window.

"You did this."

Watched as she unlatched it.

"She died because of you."

Watched as she lifted it as high as it would go.

"See what your incompetence caused?"

Watched as she crawled out onto the ledge.

"You killed her."

Watched as she looked up toward the sky.

Watched as she closed her eyes.

Tipped forward.

Fell.

YOU KILLED HER!

The mental bulwark in Giles's mind breached, and moldering darkness tumbled in to consume every last rational corner. He hardly noticed as he inched toward the very same window,

Dad standing beside him now, urging him on; hardly noticed as he opened the shutters and lifted the glass, squinting at the burst of light outside. Giles stepped onto the ledge, the wind buffeting his shirt and hair.

"Do it," said Dad. "Jump. It's the only honorable thing left for you to do."

"Yes," said Giles, his stomach twisting into knots. "Yes, this is my fault."

He glanced down at the asphalt below and wondered how badly it would hurt, if his head would splatter when it hit the ground, if the people below would hear the sound of punctured flesh and snapping bones. He didn't want to die, but Dad was right: it was the only honorable thing left for him to do.

That was when he spotted the tricycle parked outside the building.

Giles thought of Norbing, and all at once he was transported back to his first morning in Manila.

"We all do bad things," Norbing had said. "We Immortals, but we also human, and humans make mistakes. You young, you maybe too confident. So you make mistake. Now you own mistake, and you fix mistake, and next time you be careful because you remember mistake."

The memory was like a splash of cold water.

Terrified as he realized how close he'd been to ending his own life, Giles staggered back from the window, sucking in a series of shallow, rapid-fire breaths.

"What are you doing?" Dad asked, eyes narrowed.

"Finishing what I started," Giles answered.

He fell to his knees where he'd dropped the notebook and pen and snatched them up with trembling hands, embracing them like a long-lost love.

"It's too late for that," Dad admonished, but Giles wasn't listening.

He peered up at the image of the father who'd abandoned him, and for the first time in his entire life, he realized how little the man's opinion of him truly mattered. Even if the specter that stood before him were real, how exactly did that make him worthy of Giles's respect? Giles always used to believe he'd done something wrong, that it was his unknown sin that had made his father go away. He'd spent his entire life atoning for that sin, striving to become the person he thought his father would have wanted him to be in the hopes that someday, he might return. But now Giles understood the truth: The fault lay with Dad, not with himself, and there was no point in trying to make amends for someone else's failure. Norbing had been able to pursue his life's work by refusing to listen to his narrow-minded father, and now, Giles would pursue his own by doing the same.

The notebook quivered violently, but Giles tackled it to the floor and forced it open to the last partially filled page. And, as he once more fell into the rhythm of writing, he felt the creature's hold on him begin to weaken.

Dad squatted beside him in a last-ditch effort to pull his attention away.

"You're a disgrace," he spat. "If you had any honor at all, you'd accept responsibility for what you did and jump out that window."

Then the woman joined her voice with his.

"You killed me," she said, and her festering half-rotten jaw detached from her face and landed on the floor.

Giles blocked his nose from the smell, a rancid odor like months-old garbage. But he didn't take the bait. He almost had it now, and the creature knew it as well as he did.

It continued to tempt him toward despair, but with each attempt, Giles searched for another mental foothold, an anchor in the darkness. Memories of Norbing's encouraging remarks, of the Library embracing him as a brother, of Mom accepting him for who he was. Dad might not have been there to do his part, but there were so many other authority figures for him to look up to, and they had all shown him time and time again that he was loved, that he had value, and that the road to success would always be paved with failure, because that was part of the human half of his nature. Giles realized that as long as he learned from his mistakes and as long as he did his best not to repeat them, he was doing all that anyone could ever do.

At last, Giles logged one final word into the notebook. He

felt a pull, followed by a stretch. The creature released the last of its hold on the world, and Giles sensed it being plucked from the room and sucked into the notebook. The darkness faded, then dispersed.

Giles took a deep breath and let the notebook fall to the floor. There was no danger, not anymore. He closed his eyes and wiped sweat from his brow. Without the creature's darkness to smother the room and the building around it, the first darkness—the darkness that was merely an absence of light— seemed almost blinding.

Finally, after catching his breath, he capped his pen, picked up the notebook, and dropped it into his pocket. For the rest of his life he would live with the knowledge that a woman had died because of his mistake, but he would learn from it, let it make him wise and alert. That was the only way forward, the only way for him to get on with what he'd come into this world to do.

Giles rose on shaky feet, brushed himself off, and made his way downstairs.

Glossary

dai Girl

gadinamgo nga bugtaw Translates literally to "dreaming while awake." This is itself an Ilonggo translation of the Tagalog expression, *nangangarap nang gising*, which a Filipino friend provided when I asked for a decent contextual translation of the statement, "You always have your head in the clouds."

hay naku An expression of frustration or exasperation. There's no direct translation to English. In chapter 4, this is sounded out as "*hi nakoo.*"

oo Yes

salamat Thank you

sige Okay

Other Books by Jeff Coleman

Dying Breath, a short story (e-book)

Rite of Passage, a short story (e-book and hardcover)

Snapshots: The Collected Flash Fiction of Jeff Coleman, Volume 1 (paperback and hardcover)

The Others, a middle grade fantasy (e-book)

The Sign, a short story (e-book)

The Stronger Half, a novel (e-book, paperback, and hardcover)

Read a new piece of flash fiction each week for free by visiting Jeff's blog:

https://blog.jeffcolemanwrites.com/

About the Author

Jeff Coleman's passion for storytelling goes all the way back to third grade, when he wrote his first (not very good) short story about a leprechaun who enjoys eating green food. While growing up, he was captivated by classic Nintendo games like *Zelda*, and later computer games like *Myst*, each of which took place in worlds very unlike our own, and set his imagination aflame with possibilities for his own tales.

During his college years, Jeff fell in love with math, physics and philosophy, subjects that seeded his heart with a profound interest in the many extraordinary mysteries to be found in apparently ordinary things. Jeff is a firm believer that there is more to the universe than immediate appearances suggest, that there is more to our existence than meets the eye. He's therefore fascinated by stories which probe beyond surface observations, stories which attempt to explore the strange and preternatural, stories which unsettle us, which make us think, which make us question what we are and why we're here.

Some of his favorite books are *The Dark Tower*, by Stephen King; *Neverwhere* and *The Ocean at the End of the Lane*, by Neil Gaiman; *The Night Circus*, by Erin Morgenstern; *The Golem and the Jinni*, by Helene Wecker; *Daughter of Smoke & Bone*, by Laini Taylor; and *Harry Potter*, by J.K. Rowling.

www.ingramcontent.com/pod-product-compliance
Lightning Source LLC
Chambersburg PA
CBHW032051180726
48284CB00004B/1284